T0113673

The Construction Project

A Short Story

Richard A. Boehler, Jr.

authorHOUSE®

AuthorHouse™
1663 Liberty Drive
Bloomington, IN 47403
www.authorhouse.com
Phone: 833-262-8899

Published by AuthorHouse 09/09/2022

ISBN: 978-1-6655-7020-6 (sc)
ISBN: 978-1-6655-7019-0 (e)

Print information available on the last page.

Contents

Acknowledgements vii

Chapter One
The Bridge 1

Chapter Two
Mysterious Sightings 15

Chapter Three
The Spirits Arrive 26

Chapter Four
*Transport to Another Place
in Time* 40

Chapter Five
Evil Enters 61

Acknowledgements

1. **The music.** To all the band directors, at all levels of education = for leadership, guidance and experience in the "wind ensembles". Concerts were amazing and marching bands were a challenge (e.g., choreography during marching band competitions). The band members always worked hard to learn the music. The friendships and love are forever embedded in memories.

2. **The football team and weight room.** To all the coaches, at all levels of sports = for leadership, guidance and the experience of "discipline" and "teamwork". Every sore ankle, broken

bone, dislocated shoulder, bump and bruise was worth it.

3. **The United States Military.** For the topnotch, unique training of this great nation: The United States of America. All heart and soul. "Honor, Courage and Commitment". Need I say more?

4. **To the University.** For the breadth of knowledge and depth of wisdom shared through various academic curriculum. The challenges were many and the experiences gained offered a path to "higher level thinking", which is essential in this world. To the dedicated professors, assistants and all levels of staff: the diligent efforts really made a difference in many students lives. Late night labs to learn the blood flow through chambers of the human heart, dissections of dog sharks, titrations with chemicals and a variety of unique laboratory techniques taught students the "way of science" (i.e., the scientific

method). And all this is carried with each student throughout life.

5. **To all the great writers.** I always enjoyed Michael Crichton and Stephenie Meyer. Especially, Stephen King (S.K.). For leadership and the many samples of what it means to be a good writer. Specifically, the guidance of S.K. impacted me in the following way: (paraphrasing) = write a lot and read a lot. Write, even if it amounts to nothing more than a pile of **IT. Keep writing. And that inspired me to at least give it a go, utilize what I know and reach deep inside to be creative. My whole life has admired such creative leaders. The creativity is wonderful in this life, and it is also seen in great art, heard in innovative music, displayed in unique characters of movies and created within innovative science.

6. **Wisdom.** For teaching a wild child the true meaning of being humble. In teaching that a rough boy could in fact grow to be a person "they never thought he could be" = "a gentleman" (Although, always part wolf).

7. **To the mystery of "Faith".**

CHAPTER ONE

The Bridge

The bridge was located in a small suburban town. Travel from one side to the other was closed some time ago... about two years earlier. Most locals did not care much, since they were familiar with the strange happenings, in the dead of the night. If you asked any one of the local people, they would certainly say: "just as well, that bridge should stay closed forever!". It was the visitors from the "non-local areas" or just people that had once lived there, that cared. People that had some familiarity with traveling the bridge. But, no familiarity with the strange evening happenings.... In fact, the outsiders that drove into town were pissed off at the never ending construction project. It was an inconvenience to travel around the bridge. Longer, darker and windy roads with lots of uncertainty resulted from "the bridge construction project".

Madison and her friends Tyler, Angie, Tom and Stacy lived in the housing development near the infamous bridge overpass. They were not entirely sure why the bridge had been boarded up with construction signs. It looked pretty sturdy to them. It was only a tiny over pass, that ran through their suburban town. Just over a pair of train tracks.... A private road stretched under the bridge and was windy. The train tracks split through a deep pine wood forest.... The road was perpendicular to the train rails.... And, eventually branched into many other deep forest roads (with little to no lighting). Ultimately, the traveler would follow the snaking road through deep pine forest woods... At the end of the secluded main road was a large building. This building was once a popular place for kids, teenagers and adults to enjoy the newest movies... on the big screen. Although the surrounding landscape was overgrown with weeds and abandoned; the movie theater was still very much alive....

The distant suburban town of Long Island had two major academic landmarks. The first was "the University". The second was "the Community College". Randy had endured many years of study at the "University", and was now teaching biology science at the "Community College". It was good to stand in front of the pre-med, pre-nursing, pre-scientist students and talk. He was young though and that was okay.... Age was just a number. What experiences he brought to that room were helpful to the "learning process". The curriculum was nothing to joke about. In fact, it would scare even a seasoned instructor.

Walking around the room and conveying the foundational concepts was important. It was his strategy. He would start the class with fifteen minutes of open discussion. A discussion that revolved around current events. Most students that dared enroll in these types of science classes were impressive to Randy. They knew the class curriculum was tough. They wanted, they all needed... an "A". An "A" for the course would help them move to the next challenging level in a long process to become a doctor. To become a nurse. Or the average scientist!

Randy was humble. Mostly because he was natured that way (designed in that way). But, also because he had endured four to five years of intense academics up at the "University". He knew that any help, even if it was an extra "review session at night", would hopefully assist each willing student to earn the so desired course grade of an "A". The classes met late at night... a few nights, each week. And it was not all nerdy scenery. There were many "cute typed students". And as Randy walked away from the front of the room to present the course topics... he could not help but notice a student that had graduated from the University, years earlier! She had been an English major and just wanted to learn more about physiology! The problem was (at least to Randy, at that very moment....) it seemed to him, that a turquoise thong can create a distraction in such an academic environment. [it was college and there were no dress codes. In fact, the room was always so damn hot that he wouldn't be surprised if he had one day found himself in a situation where some students decided to go topless!] He walked near the distraction and closer to what seemed to be "enhanced".... Eyes forward and...back in front of the black board he stood. With chalk. He liked the traditional style of presentation. Chalk on the black board. Randy was not much of an artist, but he did venture often to draw tables and graphs with chalk. To get the students interested in the topics, he would leave some parts of the tables and graphs blank. Then would ask some to come to the board to complete the data.... it was a good academic strategy for learning.

It was his first semester at the community college. There was an incredible depth of history on campus. In fact, the building (the science labs and lecture halls) was a major landmark during the small pox outbreak. Which had occurred before his time, before his birth. However, it was the history of the building that fascinated him. A night custodian talked of ghost stories.... He would say that the building is haunted. Too many damn dead cadavers were wheeled into the classroom, located just down the hall. That was a higher leveled class, where students dissected human flesh, human tissue, human organs – in the name of science! Randy cringed at the stories. He didn't mind basic dissections. Like the dissection of a pig, of a sheep eye, of a sheep brain. But, human bodies.... Dead body dissections.... Not his area of expertise! [*Randy did believe in the after-life, and the fact that his courses met late at night during the week and always on Friday eve, did not calm his mind*].

A closet in the corner of the lab held real human skeletons! They were as real as real could get. Sort of preserved to the elements....but, wear and tear were noticeable......a full skeleton had also been donated to the lab, years back. It was of a short stature, but all the bones were intact and it was a good tool for the human connective tissue lectures/

labs. The evening was upon the class. Scheduled to 11 PM, the professor decided to let the class go fifteen minutes early. After all, it was a Friday evening and the Thanksgiving holiday was approaching. After cleaning up some of the lab sheep eye guts, left over from the dissection, Randy turned to see a group of students searching for a cell phone. The frantic student was worried that she had left it in her earlier class. The human dissection lab. Randy finished cleaning up, then brought the group of students down the hall to a dark corridor. At the end of the corridor, they got into an elevator. The elevator brought them to the basement level, where the human dissection lab was located. It was extremely dark. Not just dark. But, the dark that takes the human eye ball some time to adjust too. The groups eyes adjusted quickly to the light given off from the missing cell phone. It was at the back of the lab. Located right next to a human cadaver.

The body had a white sheet sprawled over it. Randy stopped trying to get the room lights to turn on, when he noticed the dead body lift abruptly off the table! The sheet went flying to the side and the fleshy corps found itself face to face with Randy! There was not much time to react when something like that happens in a dark room... The corpse bellowed out the sentence "where's the construction bridge?" Randy blinked. He felt the gentle hand of a female student grasping his arm. She asked if he was okay? He looked around the room, and did not see any fleshy bodies...

He brought the students out of the lab, locked the door then made his way to the faculty parking lot.... It was a dark, very cold evening. The weather had just turned from an enjoyable autumn like environment to a frigid unwelcoming winter environment.

Madison and her teenage friends liked a good snow ball fight, but did not think the winter breeze was much fun at this point in time. As the group strolled down the road, they got closer to the bridge. The "construction signs" were everywhere as they approached. Tyler opened the gate to the fenced off entrance. The group followed and walked slowly across the bridge. There were no obvious projects on the bridge, at least no open bridge parts that they noticed. Perhaps, the construction was located directly under the bridge.... As they walked, they stopped about halfway over the bridge. It was a screeching sound that had stopped the group. Sort of like a ghost-like banshee screaming into the wind. The invisible wind, flowing aggressively over the bridge structures – in the pitch-black sky. No moon was present in the sky above during this night's walk....

Madison asked if anyone had a flash light? The group did not. Not one of the teenagers had a flash light or any kind of light. The typical cell phone has a nice light. Except the odd thing (that night) was that their phones did not work while standing on this mysterious bridge! The screams increased in amplitude and surrounded the group. However, the wind carried the "chill-like screech" under where they stood. Under the structure. Madison wanted to explore. She needed to see what was under the bridge. What the "construction project" really was. And what the sounds were (where they were coming from, what was producing them and where the screeches travelled to).

They lived in a small suburban town, located some distance from New York City. This bridge was no "Verrazano" or "George Washington". The bridge they were standing on was tiny, in comparison to the great city bridges. However, it still held an enormous amount of mystery. An enormous amount of "energy". Quickly, they left the bridge and followed a path that led the group underneath the structure. The sounds stopped. Their phones worked. Tyler shined a light into the structure. As they suspected, the construction was "bull shit". This bridge had been closed for over two years and they saw no construction! What they did see though was the strangest foot prints coming out of the bridge enclosure. A group of foot prints. The prints travelled away from the bridge, down a windy road. The dirt path (road) went into the deep surrounding pine forest....

The distance between the closed bridge and the path to the forest was about fifty yards. The group of teenagers entered the dark pine forest, following the strange footprints and an odd bioluminescent glow in the distance.... As they proceeded, they noticed that some of the low forest brush was painted in a glowing yellow-green ambiance. It seemed that whatever creature was moving along the path in front of them was secreting this glow.... Perhaps supernatural? Perhaps a secretion from an unidentified alien? They really were not sure. The footprints were large and imprinted deep into the dirt. The creature was not wearing shoes or sneakers. Along the trail, about twenty to thirty minutes of walking through forest, the group came across a large structure. It was a movie theater! They were familiar with this multiplex. Many Friday or Saturday nights were spent in this theater, eating popcorn and candy.... It was late and the movie theater was just about ready to close.

The group decided it would be best to visit this theater another night. Exploration would be planned for another weekend. Right now, it was getting late and the teenagers needed to make the midnight curfew. Madison made her way back home to her dads, Professor Randy.

He greeted her with smiles and asked her not to call him professor. Mr. Dad would do! They smiled at one another and called it a night, then went off to bed....

CHAPTER TWO

Mysterious Sightings

The town had mysterious sightings the past few weeks. It always occurred in the evenings, late at night.... Typically, past mid-night. The eye witnesses swore that the people they observed were from another time and place. One witness argued that it seemed that the attire was of Egyptian origin. Another sighting documented the presence of what looked like an Egyptian mummy! There were many other descriptions and it seemed that the locations were always deep in the town forest.... That is, at first it was always in the forest....

The time went by. As time usually does. Randy continued teaching at the community college in the evenings. The topic of discussion was articulation of tendons, ligaments and muscles to human bone. The topic was fascinating to many. And not so interesting to others. The group of students assigned to the dissection lab noted that their lab practical would be too difficult. They wanted to know if the professor could arrange an after-hours study session in the dead body lab, in the basement? The professor (i.e., Randy) was always eager to do this.... The subject matter was challenging and anything he could do to accelerate the learning process was okay with him....

The study session was scheduled a week from Friday. Late in the evening, at the bottom of the dead body cadaver lab.... In the basement of the college's anatomy/physiology building. Randy and Madison were eating dinner. It was not the weekend and they enjoyed sharing time together. She was a teenager and did not really want to spend all her social time with her dad. At least, that is what she told everyone.

Randy (aka: dad) knew better. They did enjoy time together. He liked sharing some memories with her. More of an attempt to prepare her with "life's lessons". Randy tapped into his experiences, serving time with uncle Sam; as a United States Naval Reservist. He attempted and hopefully was successful in presenting the purpose of being well rounded (at least in the beginning). To build a good foundation. He would say: get involved in different areas of what interests you. Some music, some sports, etc. And she was pretty good at this. She liked dance (tap, ballet, street dancing), she even tried the saxophone for a year. But, she was still only 16 and needed more time to grow.... which she certainly would do. Randy tried to present a basic path, his path....it was not the only path for each person.... But, he felt the as Madison would grow, she would find her unique niche in life....

It was getting dark and they had finished dinner. The "teenager group" was getting together that night. Madison's friends met at her house. Randy was watching a football game when the kids arrived. They exchanged their hellos and then said goodbye - as they made their way back to the movie theater....

The teenagers began a tradition. To meet at the movie theater. To just hang out and spend time together. To do what teenagers typically do. They had fun! Not much happened in the movie theater over the next few weeks. Randy continued to meet in the evenings and decided to invite a close friend to one of the biology labs. His friend was also a professor. Her expertise, though, was not biology - per se. The expert area that Tina studied was "paranormal activity". Her first degree was in the area of biology. After graduating, she joined a quest of explorers from her church to investigate ghosts.... One thing led to another, and she became so interested in the area that she got a teaching degree and presented lectures on everything from use of the Ouija board to detection methods (use of technology) to find ghosts! Randy introduced Tina to his lab and she began her talk. The students were fascinated with the video clips she presented! The topic was intriguing....

The students left for the night. Randy and Tina stayed and talked for a while. Randy explained what had happened in the basement of this school building. Tina proposed that they go to the basement and explore. She activated her high-powered flash light, that she took from her back pack. They traveled carefully to the basement area. Immediately, she sensed paranormal energy. Randy was no expert in the area... but, he felt something.... In the corner of the room, the dead body rested in a horizontal position. A sheet that had covered the body, slid off the rigid skin. A crackling sound was heard and caught Tina and Randy's attention.... Something snapped, similar to the sound of a large tree branch breaking - deep in a quiet forest. The body fell off the table and did not move. Tina and Randy looked at each other with wide opened eyes. She grabbed his hip...."romantic enough for you, professor?" He smiled, they kissed - then left the basement....

In the College campus parking lot, Randy offered to drive Tina to her car. There were many different parking lots and parking garages located around the large community college grounds. As they drove in Randy's car, Tina asked what a professor does on a typical Friday evening...after class is over? He smiled at her and replied that he was a simple guy (surprising her, he thought). She pegged him as the "complicated type". He laughed and said for all the complex experiences and knowledge in this life, I have found ways to simplify my life (and be happy, he thought). Randy continued, I like a good movie, good music from various genres, I enjoy the saxophone, a good football game on television and the company of a good lady.... There was silence. She gently placed her arm around his arm and asked if she could spend the night with him. She suggested a good movie and a bottle of wine. They left Tina's car on campus and headed to Randy's house....

It was a chilly evening. There was no snow on the ground, but the chill was in the dark, bitter wind. There was no snow on the ground, but the chill was in the dark, bitter wind. A perfect evening for a

Ouija board session. Tina had one handy, and even if she didn't – professor Randy's daughter had one in her room. The group of teenagers gathered at Madison's house as Randy and Tina arrived in the drive way. Madison approached her dad with caution, she did not recognize Tina. Madison was protective of her dad. Even as a five-year old at a community pool, Randy was not "allowed" to talk to many females. She would throw a temper tantrum and direct his attention away from any female....

Tina was different. She introduced herself to Madison and offered her the "Ouija board". Madison and her teenage friends showed interest and marveled in the possibilities of contacting ghosts! They entered the house and found a good place to summon the dead. Randy ordered some pizzas for everyone.... During the night, the teenagers explained to Randy and Tina the happenings at the bridge construction site. One teenager, Kyle, brought some artifacts from the land. Some rocks and dirt.... Tina jumped in a was happy because she explained that if the artifact had remnants of ghost.... They would be able to contact the dead! The pizzas arrived....

It was an uneventful night, with regard to contacting a viable spirit! The teenagers left for their parent's homes and Madison said good night to her dad. She was already on her phone with her friends as she left the room. Tina smiled as she overheard Madison talk about the Ouija board. "the dial on the board moved all by itself!", she said with excitement....

Randy and Tina went to the living room, where they shared a common taste for a late-night drink. Randy enjoyed the sailor's drink, Rum. Tina asked for some vodka in juice, similar to a Bahama breeze drink. It reminded her of visiting a nice beach, somewhere in the pacific.

She thought, perhaps Oahu, Hawaii… Randy smiled. He had spent some time across the street from the Aloha Football stadium. He worked in the inspector general's office for the United States Navy. The drinks warmed their blood and they snuggled together – as music played in the background. Her eyes were inviting to Randy. It was her kind loving shine, that amazingly reached out to him and held his stare. He could not look away. And right below this angel's gleam, was a cute beauty mark on her right cheek. A special soul, with love that he was lucky to connect with. They fell asleep in each other's arms….

CHAPTER THREE

The Spirits Arrive

Tina admired Randy. He admired her. Randy admired the way Tina carried herself. She had worked diligently through doctoral studies while some of their friends had sold part of their souls for cash.... That was needed to sustain the doctoral expenses. Tina chose not to strip. Randy was the sailor type – a military guy attached to a unit with NYC detectives, undercover narcotic operatives and paramedics.

Randy had many roles. One included the medical readiness of the unit. The group liked to "party". A young guy of 18 in uniform had someperks... After arriving in many different locations (depending on the missions), the undercover secret clearance gentlemen escorted their buds to the nearest bar, dance club, live music joint and followed with a visit to the strip club – for the beer. It was always a long fucking night. Then an inspection on the flight deck of the Navy Ship, at 0700... For Randy, he was always chasing the beer....! Of course, some of the views were not too bad either.... Randy never went "all the way".

He had no reason to, with a strong conscience. But, even if he did now, would anyone really know? They were not supposed to offer such things, such as the "nipples". He guessed he was just lucky? Maybe it was his face? Or his "pheromones" that took hold of the ladies...? He really did not know. Anyway, he was only there for the beer! Okay, and perhaps a dripple of sensuality... If Randy was away from Love and Affection for too long.... Years perhaps, would anyone blame him?

Tina staying the night convinced him not to start that up again (no pun intended). It was just an erection, she giggled .... And said "an erection for the "lady"?

They left the house early the next morning, eager to visit the University. Randy wanted to show Tina something strange that had happened in the cadaver lab.... They traveled to the basement to observe the dead bodies. Tina brought the Ouija board. Madison and her teenage friends were still sleeping. Sometimes, teenagers are lazy like that! Although Randy did not recall that kind of laziness when he was that age.... The basement was dark and reeked of preserving chemicals. It was also very cold and eerie....

It was a Saturday and they did not think many people would be on campus.

Although, there were many study groups and some scheduled weekend courses.... In the cadaver lab, the same dead bodies were in the same areas – for laboratory study. But, something had changed! There were more bodies and less lab space... They could see desk full of papers, binders and study notes. A stack of textbooks caught their' eyes. It was Egyptian literature. And just as Randy and Tina noticed a pile of "Egyptian styled clothes, with gold bracelets" in another corner of the laboratory – the outer area doors opened! Quickly, Tina directed Randy to the furthest point in the lab. An office that was being used for storage. They went swiftly through the open door, then hid behind a big pile of laboratory supplies. They were hidden well. Similar to lizards blending into the natural forest....

Professor Nordstrum from the history department entered with the campus custodian. A third person entered. Randy and Tina were familiar with the campus staff (the professor and the custodian). They did not recognize the third gentleman. His appearance was very different. The uniform was of the campus police. His language was of ancient Egyptian times.... Randy and Tina were scared, but more curious. After all, they were pretty sure that no one would find them. They were blended into the lab, hidden very well....

Professor Nordstrum was the guru of history. In fact, Tina was currently enrolled in an introductory American History course. The professor typically went of on a tangent, in class lectures.... Delving into Egyptian history! Tina whispered this to Randy.... They could hear conversation about transporting Egyptian royalty. The stones and gems needed for activation of the transport was only one part of the equation.

The time and place were important... The conversation seemed to leap into astrophysics! Randy was fascinated. The place was the bridge! Somehow, the transport was being activated late in the evenings. There was a "worm hole" that brought them to Egyptian times. Or one could say that the worm hole brough Egyptian times to them!

Was this even possible? There were so many complex "theories" at University. There were so many published papers. There were even more conspiracy theories! Perhaps the conspiracies held some truth! Perhaps, with the right stones and gems. With the correct place and correct time.... A travel hole could be "activated". String theory? Maybe something else? What ever it was, something was happening in their town and at the bridge, was at the heart of it....

The police officer, custodian and professor Nordstrum left the laboratory, as they continued to discuss heading over to the bridge in the evening. The best time to leave this part of the world would be at midnight. They all agreed to have some belongings packed and ready for the trip back to Egypt. Randy and Tina waited until it was safe to reenter the main part of the cadaver laboratory. As they entered the lab, they noticed a textbook the professor had left on a desk. It had some notes scribbled. The notes included formulas for transport between "worlds". Tina quickly took out her phone and frantically snapped as many pictures of the notes as humanly possible. They left the lab, together.

The University had energy. It was the weekend and there was less energy there. However, there was still a good amount of energy. They felt it. Walking across the campus grounds, they decided to stop in the activities center for an early lunch. The cafeteria had a great selection of about six to seven different types of food to eat. Everything from traditional Italian (pizza), to deli style sandwiches and a salad bar. They decided to go with the cheeseburgers, onion rings and French fries. There was always a nice selection of daily soups to eat too! They would save that selection for another day.

Tina found a nice table with two seats overlooking the campus grounds. It was as if they were eating inside a green house. Wall to wall windows allowed the natural sunlight to enter the eating quarters.

The tables were evenly spaced, with plenty of room for the large population of students, faculty and University staff. The view was amazing. A pretty campus with a large central library that contained every textbook, every piece of literature one could imagine. The central library was one of many libraries on campus. It contained many science texts, and also had a specific library of music. The other libraries on campus were more specialized to each particular area of study. For example: there was a library in the psychology dept with those type of books. A library in the physics dept with that type of literature....

As they ate and enjoyed the surrounding view of nature... they could see squirrels running across the grounds and up the historical and beautiful large campus oak trees. Tina looked over the photos of the lab notes. It was curious to her. Some of the formulas looked familiar and other formulas were adapted. So, it seemed that the construction project was more of a transportation module!

They decided to venture back to the bridge at midnight. To see what the professor was up to. Right now, though, it was Saturday afternoon and they wanted to walk toward the music department. There were recitals for the graduate music students being performed. It was part of their curriculum. To perform on designated days, in the recital halls. There were solo violinist performing on campus today. Tina enjoyed the violin. She had played the instrument a few years, before studying paranormal activity science. She thought one day she might return to the instrument as a hobby. The recitals were amazing – the music that was played included classical genres (Bach, Beethoven and some Russian composers).

After the recitals, Tina brought Randy to a private study area. The top floor of the main campus library. It was a site to see. Not all would appreciate the mystery a library has to offer. Especially now a days, with the electronic books. It was the numerous stacks of library books.... Countless rows of shelving. And along side the shelves were cubby desks. A perfect area for private studies. The icing on the cake was the view from the top floor of the library. Seated next to each other and ready to go through the technical notes found in the dead body lab..... Tina first looked out the window. The library had ample natural light entering.... It helped add and nurture the learning environment. The top floor was probably at least ten stories high. And the view of the campus was spectacular. Even for a Saturday afternoon. They could see some students, professors and staff walking around, down below.... Inside the library, looking in toward the many book stacks were lights that faded. Faded light into the depth of books.... Offering a mysterious view of the campus learning environment.... A good place to get lost in. Tina grabbed Randy's arm and smiled. "A good place to reach second base in..." they giggled! Remembering the last time that they were in this place. Studying hard core science.... She said "of course", then giggled again!

They looked down at the photos and technical descriptions. It was physics equations. The type that would scare a first-year student away in a heart-beat. Tina was intrigued.... She had a strong foundation to physics equations..... They were opening up a "worm hole", leading into another dimension, another place in time. And from what they had already gathered (looking at all the Egyptian clothes and artifacts), it was a dimension into ancient Egyptian culture! There were too many equations to digest in one sitting. The main equation that caught Randy's eyes included the realm of thermodynamics, the properties of light and motion. These three different areas of physics encapsulated technical aspects that were being applied to the opening of a worm hole. The theory became practical somewhere in the bridge construction zone. Light traveled within the constraints of physical laws. The heat that was generated in the process of travel was distributed along a transport train. The transportation was activated using a module. People were carried in a train-like car. The formulas described an initiation sequence that eventually led to the train travelling from present day time, back into Egyptian times. The travel ended at the base of a pyramid.... Sort of a "basement", that contained another module for transport. Perhaps, the base of the pyramid could propel the train to other places in time.... Tina and Randy wondered....and tried to digest all of the technical literature. It was getting late, and they decided to head back to Randy's house. They would prepare for the midnight trip to the construction bridge at midnight. First, though, they wanted to pack a few survival items: flash lights, water and protein bars. They showered and relaxed in the den, as they continued conversation about what they might come across after travelling to Egypt... Madison and her teenage friends entered the house, looking for dinner....

CHAPTER FOUR

Transport to Another Place in Time

The group talked over the strategy to travel back in time.... The teenagers were concerned. They presented their findings from visits to the bridge.... So, they decide to postpone the travel. Tina started another Ouija session, using some of the Egyptian clothes she collected from the campus dead bodies lab.... The Ouija board seemed to move and glow in the dark, they ended the session. The teenagers started their routine sleep over, and headed into the living room – where they watched movies, ate lots of chocolate candy and stayed up late into the early morning [at least, that was their plan – they fell asleep much earlier]. Randy and Tina went to bed upstairs.... It had been a long week, and a busy day.... Tina wasn't feeling that well.... Randy ordered hot wonton soup from the local restaurant.... It was delivered within twenty minutes. Tina smiled at Randy.... He kissed her forehead and she enjoyed the soup. During the night, she embraced Randy's arm as they fell asleep. The room was dark, except for the light down the hall.... Randy usually kept the hall light on through the night. Randy was asleep when Tina woke to an odd sound at the bed's edge. It was sort of a scratching sound, followed by a click. The noise stopped for about a minute or so, then returned. As she looked toward the end of the king-sized bed, she noticed that the bed sheet was slowly being pulled down toward the floor. She tried to remember if Randy had any cats in the house...Then, the breath exhaled from her mouth was turning so cold that she began to see it! This startled her.... The sheet stopped moving, when a mummified giant stood before Tina. The facial features were distorted, and covered in dark red blood. The mummy pointed toward the dimly lit hallway.

In the hallway was what seemed to be a vision, to Tina. It was of another world. Not of present time, but of ancient Egyptian times. She could see fire blazing along dark interior pyramid halls. A group of people gathered in the pyramids – for what seemed to be a funeral.... Then the vision vanished – as often visions do. A glimpse into what should not be seen, often does not show itself for too long. The room got warmer and there was no giant mummy standing in front of the king-sized bed. Tina caught her breath and noticed that the time was 3 AM. Too early to wake anyone.... She was tired anyway, and decided to get some rest. Tina cuddled in close to Randy's bare warm skin and fell asleep for the rest of the night.

Tina woke to the scent of fresh brewed coffee. She made her way to the kitchen to meet Randy for a light breakfast and a hot cup of caffeine. They talked about Tina's dream. Or, more like a nightmare. She presented the mummy that visited her and the vision she had seen down the hall. It was brief, but it seemed so real. Tina started packing some things for the trip over to the construction bridge. Her backpack was filled with water bottles, protein bars, and flash lights. They traveled that night to the construction site. It was dark, but the surrounding forest was lit well with a full moon glow. The bridge was quiet and seemed desolate. No sign of any recent visits, no footprints and so they decided to explore the area. From what Tina had read from the technical manuals found at the University, there must be a transport area. All they could find was the bridge and construction tools.

Tina opened her backpack and turned on two flashlights. Underneath the bridge was a dark tunnel. They followed the tunnel and about half way into it.... A door was located in the cement wall. Locked and sealed, Randy used a construction tool to break the door wide open. It was a sophisticated tool (he chuckled), a strong iron crow bar easily opened the door.... Just inside the rusted, open door they found a dark stair well. The stairs descended into a deep abyss. Tina and Randy followed the stairs, together. It led them down to a basement style laboratory. At least, what seemed to them as a "laboratory". There were work benches, and conference style tables. Tina found an area to sit, after she had collected a stack of "transport manuals". Randy followed and rolled a chair close to her. She said "you see, this is all the technical formulas presented in physics class!". The only thing is that the formulas were not just presented in these manuals. These technical computations were being used in what seemed to be some sort of transportation! Randy asked where the transport had occurred and when? The diagrams revealed another chamber! A chamber that contained a shuttle like car!

Randy admired Tina's zest for knowledge. She loved it. It was similar to the satisfaction of eating good creamy chocolate, high end chocolate. Randy wasn't a picky eater. In fact, he spent a good part of his life trying to gain weight, mostly by muscle. And no matter how many meals he had ingested, his body seemed to hover around 185 pounds. It didn't stop him from excelling in the area of weight lifting. Even with a medium sized build, he was able to achieve great gains in lifting weight above his baseline 185! For example, a dude that weight 300 pounds and bench presses 315, is not that impressive at all. However, Randy weighing 185 and bench pressing over 300 pounds.... now that he was proud of!

Tina could read through those physical science manuals for hours and not blink an eye. Randy on the other hand was more into the biological sciences. Not that he didn't like physics. He did, he appreciated the knowledge too. The area of physics that interested him the most were the properties of light. That section of physics fascinated him. Tina took a liking to a more theoretical area of physics: Quantum physics, time travel! Randy thought "is this even possible?". He was familiar with all the technical formulas, after all – he invested two whole years in physics classes at University with Tina.... He understood the workings of a refrigerator, an engine, a stove.... That was everyday pragmatic application of Physics (thermal dynamics and electrical conduction, etc.).... Every day life! But, after finishing the studies of theories like "the theory of relativity", he scratched his head.... Some geeks (he recalled) spent hours in the library reading and reading.... Picking their noses and taking breaks to digest the extremely difficult concepts.... He knew this for a fact, since he was once one of those geeks! (he chuckled as he remembered many library nights.... Afterwards, he always made it a point to find a good pizza place....). Tina directed Randy down a dark corridor, which led to another passageway! And behind another secret door was a long dark descending path.... They followed it together – hand in hand. Tina led with her bright flash light. Randy could hear the sound of rushing natural water on the other side of the hall wall, as they descended. He was thinking of Tinas sparkling brown eyes.... She was angelic to him and to the world... He was a lucky guy to have connected with such an angel.... He was thinking that they needed a "song". And what came to mind immediately (as if it were written in the stars) was the Van Morrison song: "Brown Eyed Girl".

He would present that to her, next time they were cuddling to pillow talk. The song would symbolize her angelic eyes (of course), and it would remind him of their sort of unofficial (and perhaps official, he would have to ask her....) anniversary date. For him, Randy thought it was January 17th! They reached the end of the descending path about twenty minutes into the walk. Tina arrived at a modern styled looking door (which was odd, since the environment up to this point was more stone and barbaric in view). The door had a sensor that immediately opened as they approached.... After entering, the door closed and they found themselves in a clean room style laboratory. And, at the other end of the large room was a pristine looking transport car! They had found what they were looking for. Before, entering the car, Tina sat at a table and reviewed the technical manuals. Randy followed and asked if it was really even possible to travel from point A to point B, when point A was present day and point B was Egyptian times! Tina smirked and said: "absolutely! Why not?". They looked at each other with excitement and fear of the unknown.... They weren't familiar with the energy source that propelled the car into another place in time. But, the instructions were pretty clear. And there they were, in the car – ready to go.... The underground bunker, where they started travel from, opened up and ascended.... They could feel the incline, it was significant.

However, surprisingly their ear did not "pop". The dark surrounding environment opened to a clear tube that they could see right through. And darkness turned to "light". It was fascinating to Tina and Randy. They supposed that it would have been fascinating to anyone riding in that car! Outside the tube they could see a clear and crisp blue sky – as far as the eyes could possibly see. The travel was smooth, they did not feel any bumps in the rails (if that was what they were traveling on). The technical manuals described what seemed to be some sort of railway system, and perhaps it opened into what was theoretically speaking.... "worm holes". Breaks in time, breaks in dimensions.... Where, if done correctly, could in fact bring a traveler to a distinct place/time in history....As they traveled, they noticed that watches and electrical devices (their phones) stopped working. The shuttle slowed and light turned to darkness. They had arrived! The car door opened and in the distant they observed a dimly lit "cave". Fire torches lined the distant tunnel and they followed.... Prior to exiting into the dark abyss, Tina looked over the dash board. The manuals she had read showed good information about "time", "distance", "acceleration", etc. Her experience in physics helped her understand the technical formulas that were applied to this travel. Force equals "mass" x "acceleration". DV = NRT, where constants were inserted into the equation and "D" (distance) was calculated. The numbers were not simple to understand and another obstacle was always converting the units correctly.... From her view point, after digesting all the technicalities.... They were somewhere in ancient Egyptian times....

The cave was dark and damp. They could hear the sound of water on the other side of the rock formations. The path led them to another area. A room, with a door on the far side of the wall. The door was curiously modern in style and in fact looked to be "French". Randy knew something of designs.... Especially, when it had to do with France. He took years of French and loved the language. The food was good and the French wines were outstanding! Tina laughed and said only you would point that out! She hugged him. He said see the two doors that are symmetrical? That's a cool style! They entered the next room and were surprised to see that is was more of a temporary housing unit. There was a kitchen area, a living room area with television and furniture, and a bedroom area with bathroom and shower. It seemed odd to Tina, since she thought for sure they were in Egypt. However, at the other side of the room (across from the kitchen) was a clear wall. Looking through the clear wall, they could see a vehicle. It was another transport module. Before venturing off, Tina decided it would be a good idea to rest. There was plenty of food that they prepared for a good diner! They showered and went to bed. On the bedroom wall was nice art. A large painting of what looked to be Hawaii! The painting had incredible detail, with pretty colors. The ocean was crystal blue and the coral was bright orange. Tina and Randy admired the painting. Randy nibbled gently on her soft skin, around her neck. She purred and asked what he was thinking about? He said, maybe one day we can vacation in Hawaii? Then paused, and said or one day honey moon there.... She turned and embraced his lips in hers.

Her lips tasted like vanilla and strawberry (it must have been her lip gloss!). There was more. It wasn't just lip gloss flavoring.... No, it was more of a natural taste. A sweetness, an angelic babe like sweetness.... Time and distance stopped. There was no time, there was no distance between Tina and Randy.... And it started with the passionate kissing of their lips.

Her tongue entered his mouth, and he followed her lead.... Tina admired Randy's tongue. It was unique – a twist of technique from many years of playing a saxophone.... A soft and sensual tongue that reached her most intimate places.... Tina's tongue was the hottest and most sensual feeling he was greeted with, and she knew it! She winked at him as she retracted her tongue from his mouth (just to catch some breaths...). And a few more winks at Randy was followed by Tina pressing her body on top of Randy's. He wasn't sure where her shirt disappeared to..... and his thoughts did not last long on that subject. She was wearing the cutest bra he had ever laid eyes on.... (She had a cute collection of bras).

Tina and Randy were similar. A lady and a gentleman. They appreciated each other's connection of the "soul", the connection of the "mind", the connection of their "love". Randy admired Tina's loyalty, her brilliant light, her funny sense of humor and her pretty shining eyes.... Tina had a similar feeling toward Randy.... He always offered "honesty/loyalty", "love and affection", "understanding". They were soul mates.... Tina could do no wrong (not in Randy's eyes). She could do no wrong this night (in their heat of passion), and could do no wrong in this life (Randy adored her, and could not explain it because it was something that words could not describe.... His heart and soul immediately gravitated near Tina – from day one, from minute one, from second one....). Tina was angelic, a little piece of heaven on Earth.... It was a night of peace and serenity – as they fell asleep in each - other's arms....

The next day, Tina woke to the scent of fresh brewed coffee! They ate breakfast in the kitchen and talked about travel to Egypt. Randy felt that there was something sinister happening in these tunnels.... It was sort of a sixth sense, a gift or a curse. He didn't believe they were traveling to Egypt at all. Tina asked where he thought they were travelling too? He paused and held his hand near his chin.... Deep in thought. He was thinking that this may be some portal to Hell! She could see his expression and did not disagree with him. Tina only said that she hoped he was wrong. Randy quickly agreed with her.... There was a loud sound in the distant room, on the other side of the wall. The sound was an arriving vehicle. They could hear the pressure change in the distant room. Randy and Tina quickly found a good place to hide. And just in time, as a group of people entered the living room area.... Tina recognized a staff member from the University, a custodian and an office worker. The group of people could not see Randy and Tina. The custodian was dragging what appeared to be a dead body along the floor boards....

Tina presumed the body was dead, since it was stiff as a rod. The skin appeared grey and there was a wound on the upper temple, in the head. The group sat at the kitchen table and began to eat. Something did not seem right with the group, though. Tina could see a red glow in the custodian's eyes. Perhaps, Randy was correct about the transport to "Hell". The custodian seemed evil and since he was dragging a dead body – Tina figured he was certainly a murderer. The evil group left the kitchen area, dragging the dead body. Within minutes, they were transported back to the construction bridge area. Tina and Randy quickly entered the next tram area. Within minutes they left for what they thought was "Egyptian Times". The transport was not long, in fact they were surprised at their surroundings.... As they exited the car, they found themselves in a tomb room.... The walls were stone, with Egyptian like symbols engraved into them.... Tina was familiar with the symbols. The writing presented a story of the bodies buried there. There was also writing of devil worship. Tina believed that they were not in a typical Egyptian tomb. She believed, after reading more of the writings, that they were in a tomb of criminals. The tomb had evil in it, and had some odd-looking statues. The statues kept the evil within a certain circumference....

Tina reached into her backpack and pulled out two flash lights. The room was dark and only lit with wall torches. In the distance Tina could see what seemed to her as a "shadow" moving.... She could see the shape of a mummy, with bandages. As the two walked closer, they could feel a drop in temperature. The breath was seen coming out of their' mouths.... Then it went away. The room warmed and the shadow was gone. Tina held Randy's hand and strongly suggested that it was time to leave this tomb. She sensed evil, she sensed death.... They decided to regroup, and returned to Randy's house – where the "teenagers" were eating pizza and playing with a Ouija board.... The night was interesting, with the summoning of spirits from the dead. However, the teenagers had no luck and decided to retreat to Madison's bedroom. Tina and Randy were tired. They decided to relax in the upstairs bedroom.... Tina was beginning to stay the night, more often and Randy was happy. There were so many things that made him happy (he was thinking, as she took a shower). Her sense of humor was definitely ranked up in the top five qualities of this savvy lady.... It was different. Randy liked that. He was thinking about how it was different. Sort of dry humor with a bit of sarcasm.... And deep in the humor was a flash of brilliance!

It had him thinking (often), "did she just really say that", "where did that come from?". A cute style, that he loved.... But, he was still learning more about her.... And that was ranked up there in the top five qualities! She had hobbies, she loved to be involved in different things – and sometimes be involved in nothing at all! Which was a pretty cool combination of qualities (if that made sense, he was thinking maybe he should stop thinking and just relax!). Tina slipped into satin lingerie, while Randy took a quick shower and returned to her.

CHAPTER FIVE

Evil Enters

They found themselves back at University. The staff lounge was impressive. It had coffee machines, vending with plenty of sugar. There was also a pretty good selection of healthy snacks and food. Tina brought the manuals, from travel to Egypt. The thing was, she was beginning to think that it was not Egypt. It was becoming evident that where they traveled to was more of a place that people would call "Hell". Randy remembered the glowing red eyes of the custodian. Tina remembered how the group dragged a dead body along the floor, with no emotion....

Evil does not present itself with such clarity, though. More often, it is the evil that presents itself through "niceties" (being too nice and too kind) that was more of a concern to Tina and Randy. The custodian, the professor and the cop had been inserted into the community decades earlier. Perhaps, even longer. And they were a perfect trio of evil. The cornerstone of a local suburban community.... Randy made a fresh pot of coffee, and found a salad in one of the vending machines. He brought the lunch over to Tina.... As they ate the chicken salad, Tina sketched a time-line on paper. It was clear that a pattern was beginning to emerge.... Evil was getting sloppy and in time, Tina hoped that someone would put a stop to it. It was more than the round of the mill disagreement. It was more than an argument, more than different opinions, or different ideals, different social classes.... Sadly, what Tina and Randy had stumbled upon was a "way of life within an evil community". The way of life was filled with "mysterious accidents", "mysterious deaths", and was rooted in pure evil. Randy had some theories that he presented to Tina. The first theory was that the custodian was simply "the devil" or maybe "a son of the real devil" (the real devil most likely lived deep in the heat of the earth, which was Randy's second theory). He continued.... The professor and the cop were not human. And more than evil. Randy swore that he observed qualities of wolf and vampire.... [that was his third and fourth theory...].

Tina moved closer to him and gently kissed his neck.... Followed with a sensual hug. And paused.... She whispered: "so, do you have a cross and silver bullet?". They smiled at each other, and he thought – she has an incredible sense of humor with a splash of brilliance (he loved that about her....). They decided to take a break. Tina and Randy left for an afternoon of bike riding around campus.... It was a perfect day to enjoy time together.... The day was good, with a perfect breeze and spring-like seasonal temperature. Riding through the wooded University bike trails always fascinated Tina and Randy. It could best be explained as travel into an enchanted forest. A forest filled with dips and incline, but smooth black toped paths. Guiding through each wooded path, they came across buildings. Academic structures for lectures, for laboratories, for research, for libraries. Each area designated for a certain area of study. They were approaching the biological sciences area, which had a natural fresh water lake – situated in between freshman dorms. Within the lake, Tina observed turtles. Randy could see a school of tropical fishes, brightly colored orange.

As they traveled, the two could hear nature all around. The silence of the forest, the chirping of birds, the sound of fresh breeze making way through tree canopies…. [Randy followed Tina through the various campus bike paths, mostly in silence. He thought of a recent weekend trip to the beach…. As he smiled, he first thought of the rest area they had stopped at – to grab a cup of coffee] Before leaving the car to enter the rest area building, they observed a couple in the distance. A Chinese guy with his girlfriend. She was pretty - with long dark hair, to the length of her hips. Her hair was exotic, and very beautiful. Tina hit Randy on the shoulder for looking… he smiled at Tina and said what came to mind…."her hair is beautiful, exotic - yes! But, there was no comparison to your hair and your style. Randy reminded Tina that his heart melted (always) just at the thought of her pretty thick, Italian hair - how pretty it was as it shined in the sunlight and how exotic looking and stylish (with length to her lower back) it was to him! She was an elegant, olive-skinned Italian lady with the most amazing hair he had ever seen – or would ever see. And he just continued to smile as he thought of that moment in time. They left the rest area and traveled to a beach community, within walking distance to the Atlantic ocean....]. Tina stopped Randy, they were approaching a dip in the bike path that was tapped off with construction area signs.... [The motel was a simple structure, only with two floors. Their room was spacious, with nice wooden flooring. Entering the room, they got the feel of "the beach". It had white walls, a king-sized bed with some basic furniture - including a desk and a television. The far wall was not a wall at all, it was a large double doored glass door! Randy immediately opened the door and fresh ocean air rushed into the room!

The air outside was so fresh and filled with the sounds of a beach community. Being so close to the ocean, the breeze was constant and brought waves upon waves of various sounds. For example, the flag pole, located outside the motel made a constant chiming sound as the metal flag clips banged against the iron flag pole. It was a reminder of the ocean breeze, blowing along and being absorbed by surrounding structures.... Randy and Tina unpacked their weekend travel bags, took a shower – then found peace and serenity for an afternoon – napping next to one another in the king-sized bed. The peace and serenity was guaranteed in a place like that. The fresh ocean breeze continued to rush into the room, in waves. While, Randy and Tina napped within loving embrace – the door stayed open. Randy could hear

Tina's heart-beat. Tina whispered to him, in private, reminding him that she would always be there for him to take care of him with her genuine love and devotion...... he kissed her softly on her cheek....and as he absorbed her exotic vanilla scented perfume, he thanked her, kissed her again.... Then repeated the devotion and love back to her, ... To his soul-mate....]

There was something strange about the construction area. It reminded Tina of the construction found at the local bridge. Tina and Randy left their bikes on the side of the path and started walking toward the construction site.....And as they entered the construction area, a path led to tunnel. Tina turned on her cell phone flash light and continued into the tunnel. Randy followed, closely. About twenty minutes into tunnel, they came to a closed iron door. Randy was able to get the door open, and they entered the dark room. After flipping the light switch, Tina was surprised to see a modern styled laboratory. At the far end of the room, they observed a similar transport module car. As the custodian entered the dark Egyptian tomb, the cop and evil professor followed. The cop was dragging a body of a man that seemed barely alive. But, he was alive. He needed to be alive for the "transfer of energy to occur". In the dark tomb, of criminals.... was a secret. A secret ritual that was carried out by the custodian. He was no mere custodian, though. Some would call him by his name: the devil. Or perhaps there was a higher order of "devil". A "supreme devil" that sent the "custodian" as the "son of the devil", to Earth. What these evil creatures were doing in the dark tomb, was bringing life back. A victim was needed. The life, the soul, the beating heart was needed to be transferred into the mummified criminal Egyptian body. And, after the successful ritual was performed. The "victim" died. The Egyptian mummy was brought to life and brought through the transport car to the University....

Tina and Randy were back in Randy's house. The teenagers were doing what teenagers do on Friday evenings.... Pretty much, nothing.... And that was a point in their lives they would look back on and realize, it wasn't so bad. The weeks went by fast and the season changed into warmer summer. Strange occurrences began to be noticed around the suburban Long Island Town. More and more murders were happening. At least, that is what the "public thought". Tina and Randy knew better. They had followed the tracks back to Egypt many times and were more familiar with the facts.... Innocent people were targeted, brought to the dark Egyptian chamber and killed. One murder seemed more grotesque, when compared to the others.... (if that were possible). The transfer of energy on that particular night was to bring back a dashing princess. Not the typical princess. More like a princess of the criminals that had been buried in the Egyptian tomb. She was powerful, though. And the custodian devil took an immediate liking to her. As the weeks went by, the devil conspired with her at the University.... The darkness grew....

Tina and Randy knew that it was time to put an end to the evil. They met with the local church. It was evident to Tina that what was needed were "tool of the church". A blessed container of water; "holy water". A blessed rosary. And a blessed bible with cross. And they were ready to attack the evil. Randy figured that if he could take out the custodian, that would put an end to the evil followers (the cop, and the professor). Tina was concerned about the Egyptian princess. For one thing, Tina did not like her – simply because she had jet black slick hair to her waist. She was pretty. She was also evil. Randy smirked at Tina. And added to her discussion. "isn't that often the case with evil?" Tina was curious, often the case? Randy continued. It is just that, when you think about it.... evolution is real. We have evolved to be a good species. Very human! However, did you ever think about what has also evolved? I mean, as good evolved and matured.... did you ever think that the "not so good" have evolved too? And they had evolved. It simply was "Good verse Evil". Not your run of the mill disagreement. Randy was referring to pure evil that would commit the most devilish crimes; including poisoning, and cold-blooded murder! In the mind of the custodian, the devil's son.... Causing an illness (cancer through poison exposure.

Sometimes the evil in the community targets the pets of people they didn't like or their own pets to seem like they were the "victims"…. This type of evil was no victim, but is very cunning…. The evil custodian would poison a dog, poison a cat…. Then see if the dose of poison was enough to cause cancerous tumors….), causing a lethal car accident (a mysterious car accident that seemed coincidental; although it was not), or thinking up some evil plot that a normal person could not think of was "justified". In the devil's senses – it was a reaction to good. Perhaps, just that he did not care for the "spirit of good". The "good people" living their lives, building their' lives through work, education, gained experience and most importantly building the foundational blocks for a good family (wife, husband, kid(s))…. The devil did not appreciate this. There was an incentive for him to "destroy" what was "built by good people". And the effects of destruction; misery, sadness…. well – that made the custodian "happy".

Tina and Randy were eating breakfast together.... With good cups of freshly brewed coffee. It was an amazing night. They could hear the teenagers practicing the Ouija board in the downstairs living room, while watching "scary movies". Randy and Tina were upstairs making love – and it truly was amazing. She had a way about her.... A peace and serenity that reached the heavens.... Randy was thankful to be her life long partner [no, not just partner.... Friend, lover, future husband, future dad....]. And they were trying to conceive.... through pure love for one another.... The birth of a child is a blessing from the heavens......Tina and Randy knew that. Randy believed that.... [he was not the most religious gentleman on this planet...]. However, he was given some gifts (early on, as far back as he could remember....) that enabled him to see some vision.... vision that was from another place, and sometimes another time.... It was a great thing.

It was a burden, a curse – he thought sometimes...... Under the blanket, she pressed her soft-moist lips to Randy's lips. She kept the lips there with a gesture of sensuality, complete focus, complete love – and in the feeling of pressed lips together.... Tina and Randy felt pure trust, honesty, loyalty.... it was amazing, what they could feel, just with the touch of two lips! It was always amazing to each of them, that all the things that were important in a relationship was communicated. Were communicated without words! The communication was heavenly, and it was true. Later that night, they talked about baby names. It was an exciting topic. Of course, there were the top 100 baby names of the present year. Randy smiled and felt that Tina would be great at selecting the best baby-name that could be selected! Unless, there were twins.... Then they would need two baby names.... He smiled at her again and asked if twins ran in her family. Twins were in his family..... (the family from his early years.... Some good years and lots of not so good years.... The previous family he was raised in, along with the wolves, bears and monsters of his upbringing.... He thought silently....and remembered that along the way, even after childhood.... There were many monster-type events he experienced, that he would never be able to completely get rid of – although he wanted to.... But, then he thought that all of it made him into the gentleman he was today.... Not perfect, but as close to "good" as he could be, with an eye to get better, where he could...).

The summer was around the corner, and the town began reporting more murders. At first, the occurrences seemed "random". But, as the town entered into the summer season – the string of events could not be ignored. Randy and Tina found more Egyptian artifacts, and plenty of clothes. The literature from the transport areas shed light into what they had stumbled upon.... Deep in the local town grounds, was a carnival.... a place where people gathered to enjoy a night out.... And this one particular night proved to be filled with a fearful event – another victim was captured.... The victim was dragged from the carnival to the parking area. Tina and Randy followed, as they travelled into the nearby wood (which coincidently, was at the construction bridge location). After some time, Tina and Randy were back in the dark tomb of Egypt. They were able to hide in the near distance, as the ritual began. It was clear (to them) that the ritual resulted in an immediate transfer of energy. The criminal was transferred into the victim! The group left the dark tomb, after the ritual was complete. Randy and Tina were about to leave the tomb, when they heard foot-steps in the dirt.... It was the dark haired princess.... She had remained in the tomb and found Randy with Tina! Tina quickly grabbed holy water and lunged at the dark-haired woman! The lady pleaded to stop and explained that she was not evil at all! They had made a mistake and brought back the wrong energy! She was trapped in a circle of evil, close to the devil custodian.... and feared that he would find the truth about her.... Randy and Tina discussed their revised "plan". They now needed to follow this princess. She would bring them to the devil's chamber...where they would send him back to where he belonged (to the depths of hell). There was not much time to discuss, since the custodian was well aware of their' plot to target him. After all, he did have some evil powers that they did not understand. Nor, would they really want to understand if they even could.... The custodian smirked at all three of his soon to be "victims". And in a flash, they were brought immediately to the dark surrounding dessert. The power of this devil was evident and it shocked Randy and Tina. Within minutes, the dessert sand created a storm that inhibited their ability to see into the distance. The three walked forward, as best they could. The storm calmed (somewhat) and located directly in front of them.... Was a mountain. The terrain was gradual and there were clear levels. They would have to climb each level (and most likely be approached with challenges at each level). The dark haired princess advised them to rest.... She wanted to present her familiarity with this world. She needed to advise tina and randy of the evil that existed in this mountain, some challenges she was aware of and ultimately – how to defeat the devil – who was located at the very top of the mountain....

This slick black-haired princess was good. She was wise beyond her years. Randy and Tina were intrigued will her presentation. She was passionate about the topic and well versed in the details. Randy thought there was more to this Egyptian lady than he knew. She was mysterious and he wanted to find more information about the happenings, surrounding the pyramids. But, that was for another place and time (if they survived these soon to be devilish challenges). The devil was not the all-mighty devil. There were others. He was just a follower.... and, strong creative though. He could appear anywhere he wanted and delved into the dreams of unsuspecting victims. Of course, the dreams were always presented as a good omen – the devil made sure of that. The time factor would certainly impact their feelings. Tina asked what the time factor was. It was similar to being apart from someone you loved for a long period of time. Good souls feel an impact on time. Minutes apart seemed like hours. Hours seemed like days. Days seemed like weeks, and so forth. It was cruel.... And went against the laws of nature.... This time factor will be used to distort present day and it will have a negative impact on the mind.... The evil creature will also go after the heart and even the soul. The heart will be effected in a negative way.... Where the victim will change for the worse....

The mountain was ominous, and dark.... They began to climb. Within minutes Randy noticed a mist in the distance. And as it approached, the group could see flashes of light and hear crackles of thunder from within.... Tina grabbed Randy by the hand – but, was shocked to feel his body pulled violently from her grip. He was sort of sucked into the mysterious mist and disappeared! She yelled for him, with no response.... Only the sound of thunder and the flash of lightning – from within.... Tina turned to run from the mist, with the black-haired princess.... They too, were sucked into the mist – violently. Randy found himself at the top of the mountain, in a dark cavern – surrounded by candle, fire, wet cavern stench and what looked like snake headed women.... They were guarding the devil's son – the evil custodian. Randy quickly opened his back pack and found some handy items (holy water, a knife, a holy cross...).

Tina and the black-haired princess found themselves in another level of the mountain. Within seconds, no within the time it takes a heart to beat – Tina was viciously attacked by the "good black-haired princess". She was not good – it turns out that she was out for blood and she was going to take it from Tina.... They wrestled, and Tina was over powered by the dark-haired evil force.... The cross around Tina's neck glowed a bright white iridescent color.... It startled the evil beast and she disappeared.... That bought Tina some time to pull out holy water from her pocket, and a rosary.... She prayed, and just in time to complete a one "our father" and one "hail-Mary", when the dark creature lunged at her – again....

Pulling her hair and scratching the side of her face.... [Tina remembered her training, remembered the things that were important for battling "evil".... if she could wrapped the rosary around this dark haired beast neck and pour the holy water down her throat, she just might have a chance to make it home]. The creature continued to wrestle tina on the ground with relentless strength.... A force of a crazy person, the force of some adrenaline junky, the force of evil.... The rosary caused a burning singe around the beasts' neck, followed with the screaming that pierced the ear drum of Tina! She quickly emptied all of the holy water into the creatures' throat.... When a flash of light burst out of the area.... The black-haired princess was not there. The remnants of her body were only ash and dust. Tina fell down and tried to catch her breath. She thought it was just the adrenaline rush, after being attacked.... Something didn't seem right to her....

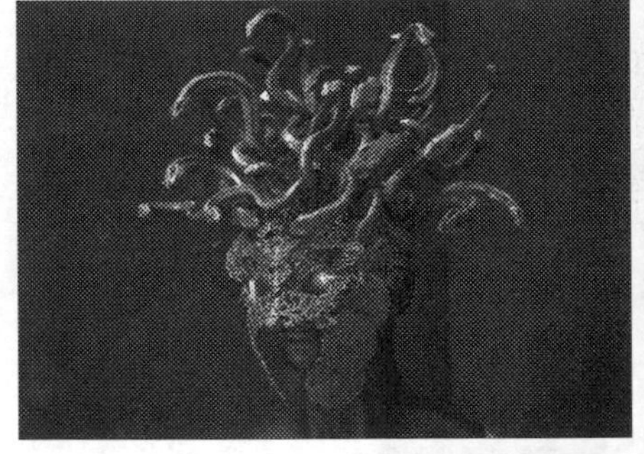

Randy stood idle, at the top of the mountain – surrounded by a group of snake-headed women. Even in the face of adversity, he kept his humor. {Randy thought to himself – some of these women look cute! Minus the snake heads, of course.... that is, until the group of women changed from a state of "cute" to the real beasts that they were!}. The devil is not as strong as people make him out to be. It is not the true strength or the true force of evil that is direct in this world.... It is more of the "indirect" nature of evil that causes the suffering and sadness. Indirectly, the devil has a way of "influencing" the weak. Not only this group though. There are just soulless individuals that rise to the occasion, too. As far as these medusa looking creatures, he was not too concerned. Flush with his muscular leg, was a nice sized silver knife! Along with a decade of training and with the force of good on his side – Randy removed the knife from its holster and started a direct assault on each creature. The stabbing was effective and efficient, with precise slicing along the throat line – to remove each head. A dark green acidic blood flowed from each severed head, as the bodies lay life-less on the dark cavern ground.

This angered the devil! Randy grinned. The cave lit up with the fires of hell and the devil appeared. Randy was thrusted violently back into a burning wall of fire! [during time of tragedy, during time of war – the soldier makes peace with his maker. And Randy had that conversation years earlier.... In the depths of hot fire, he returned to that place and time – the conversation with a force so awesome – so magical that words would not describe it accurately.... He was here – completing the prayers and conversation – with the feeling of a weight being lifted off his chest.... It was a good feeling but not a feeling that lasted long. It was just an awareness that he had made peace with his maker.... And, that harms-way was no longer a threat to him and all that made their final peace....]. the devil was good at creating chaos. And where randy was sent was just that. An area of death. Engulfed in the dark cavern with a ring of fire. And in the heated surroundings, Randy grabbed on to the "blessed cross". The cross offered protection, a cooling film – a cooling shield around him. As randy walked through the fire, he examined the devil – and grinned. The devil laughed, and was ready to attack. Randy proceeded to lunge forward inserting a hot silver knife deep into the devils throat! Randy twisted the blade, and left it in place. What followed, sealed the deal. Randy quickly grabbed the devils-head and snapped it off! The energy of the devil, of course, remained – fleeing out of the body back into the depths of hell. The mountain disappeared, and the mist brought Tina to Randy. They embraced each other and cried. Somehow, they had made it back to the transport and returned home – together....

Randy and Tina rested, at home – they were happy to be together, they were exhausted from the battle. Randy fell asleep, peacefully next to his lover – next to his soul mate. Tina stayed awake, watching Randy. Observing him, closely.... She turned off the lights. The wall mirror, located directly across from their bed reflected the indirect evil glow of Tina's eyes.

The End.

Printed in the United States
by Baker & Taylor Publisher Services